Creatures

Christopher Ridge

Published by Christopher Ridge, 2023.

CREATURES

First edition. March 19, 2023.

ISBN: 979-8215767214

Written by Christopher Ridge.

Table of Contents

Welcome to a small collection of creature stories. In here you will find creatures in space, creatures out at sea, creatures in the jungle, pretty much, creatures just about everywhere of various types. Some are gory, some light-hearted but they all are about creatures. There is also a giant bug story included. After all, what would a small collection be without a giant bug tale or two?

Hope you enjoy.

Special thanks for use of the photo to Latoscuro@morguefile.com

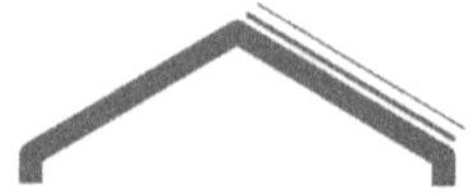

TITAN BEETLE REVENGE

Bob Clark couldn't believe the size of the thing as it towered over the sub-division which were once cornfields.

Cookie cutter houses he called them because they all looked the same.

The first thing that crept into his mind when he saw it was that he was getting way too old for killing bugs and rats.

Shoulda quit this job back when he was thinking about that desk job at the truck company. But that wouldn't have been any easier either. The idea of being stuck in the same office as the branch manager filled him with disgust and hatred.

His body wasn't quite what it used to be. Thanks to a stroke, he lost vision in his left eye. Most recently his left leg because of a fight with a giant rat two years ago when the crazy critter bit it off. He can still see the large yellow chisel teeth sinking into his flesh and severing his leg as if it were nothing but a toothpick. The way it twitched its nose and its bloody whiskers. But at least he did manage to get a grenade down its throat and watch it erupt into a fiery mist of carnage and hair. He even saw his leg flying in the air and landing somewhere in the distant woods.

He balanced himself on the crutches and squinted his eye as he observed this large beetle creature and wondering how he was going to exterminate this thing.

Its eyes as big as houses and glowing red as they rotated around surveying the neighborhood.

He'd heard stories about this beetle in the past but thought they were all myths.

Humorous myths made up from various exterminators about large beetles showing up, devouring houses, and tearing stuff up.

Sure. Like the giant rat was supposed to be a myth too.

Then later came the giant ants. And let's not talk about the humongous centipedes.

At the time it sounded very silly. Too silly to believe. It was known as the worst apocalypse ever.

The beetle appeared out of nowhere towering over the mountains and trees and standing high above the clouds. It didn't even seem to be in physical form but more like a ghostly apparition.

Before it would appear, a loud screech could be heard from miles away and sounded like it was coming from the sky.

They thought the sounds were coming from God himself. People were running and screaming calling it the second coming.

It was the second coming all right but was a far cry from God. So, any sinners left that needed to do some repenting still had some time. At least this time around.

Dark clouds quickly rolled in and gathered in large masses as if the devil himself formed them. The beetle toyed with people as if to say, 'watch what I'm going to do. Y'all be looking out down there.'

The earth thundered and shook causing the ground to split open in large channels. Houses collapsed and fell into the dark abyss along with people. Car horns blared as the roads rose high as if something was underneath pushing them up. Concrete dust shooting like a geyser in Yellowstone State Park.

Houses and bridges falling into the craters. People screaming, waving, and kicking as their feet searched for solid ground.

Of course, none of this would be complete without the news anchors trying to get as much footage as possible, each trying to deliver the next story that is going to make them famous.

Bob shook his head in disgust and couldn't help but laugh as he watched some idiotic camera man getting shots of the beetle up close and personal. So personal the beetle swept him up in its mandible and shoved him and his camera in its mouth.

"Hope he enjoys the ride into the gullet," Bob chuckled. Maybe one day the beetle will crap out that camera and his trip would be found footage like the Blair Witch Project.

He propped up the hoodie on his jacket to shield himself from as much of the rain as possible. It was coming down like bullets and the sky was completely black. The tornado alarm cut like a knife causing his ears to ring.

The beetle's shiny carapace, black like obsidian stone, moved back and forth in a rhythmic motion as if out on a quest.

It was. Its mission was to destroy everything in its path and it was doing a good job of it.

He watched as the beetle's mandibles cut through the houses like paper sending them into splinters and leaving in its wake nothing but a pile of timbers and screaming victims waving bloody arms underneath a near impossible pile of rubbish that was going to take days to clear out.

The air smelt of moisture and mildew, an odor given off from the beetle, and every now and then it would screech. He never knew beetles made this type of sound. It was disturbing and made goosebumps creep around his neck. It sounded loud and echoed like a tornado alarm.

After today there was going to be a lot of empty lots.

A lot of bodies.

A lot of blood.

The beetle swept up a man in its vice-like mandibles while he was pedaling as fast as he could to get away. The mandibles closed in tight cutting his body in half squirting blood as if the old man was nothing but a fruit gusher snack.

Henry, an exterminator back in the day, was standing in front of the beetle spraying it with a pesticide but Bob knew it was useless because there wasn't enough toxicity in the chemical to kill it.

The beetle swept Henry up as if he were nothing and chewed vigorously. An arm fell from its mouth and landed in front of Bob. On the severed arm the Timex watch was still ticking.

Bob chuckled at the thought of the old commercial. Bad timing but still worth a chuckle.

He watched as people, mostly rednecks who'd been drinking too much beer, came out with guns and started shooting at the Beetle. The bullets ricocheted off its shell-like steel. They shot and spat their tobacco as they emptied what little ammo they had.

Then you could always tell the survivor type coming out of their bunkers and tossing hand grenades at the creature. Such a tiny explosion for such a large creature.

Bob had no idea how he was going to even attempt to exterminate this thing. It had to come from somewhere.

Was there a nest of these things hiding somewhere?

Surely it didn't just materialize out of the sky.

His question was followed by another screech. And minutes later people were running from across the street as another beetle ripped up the neighborhood. People ran as the beetle followed them with its snapping mandibles. Mandibles hungry for flesh.

Human flesh.

Some people made it, and some didn't.

Another screech as another appeared. This was followed by another. It seemed there was no end to the beetles. Bob realized there had to be a nest somewhere.

Bob returned to his Ford pick-up and turned on the radio. Reports were coming in from all over the world of beetle attacks.

As if they were coming from another planet.

"It's God's curse on the world!" An old woman screamed. Placing judgment for all our sins. This is not the end but only the beginning. Repent now you sinnnnnners... God have mercy on our souls."

The rest of her speech was interrupted when she was swept up by a beetle. Still blabbering as the beetle shoved her in his mouth.

Another crazy citizen stood in the middle of the road confronting a beetle with a bible trying to exterminate it by demanding it leave this world now and go back to hell where it came from.

Of course, Bob thought, nothing like this ever happens when you really need it to. He had to admit the guy gave it his best shot.

Bob decided it was time to break out his exterminating machine.

It was time to call it out. He'd been working on the machine ever since the rat chewed off his leg. He needed something he could get around quickly in and do some damage on these bugs.

He opened the shed door and uncovered the machine. GIANT BEAUTY was written on the side with an emblem of crossbones and sculls. Don't Tread on Me was written underneath the crossbones.

The giant four-wheeler was made of steel and three times the size of a pickup truck with oversized steel belt tires. A 50 cal. was mounted on the hood with the trigger end going through his windshield where it was within reach. The windshield had been replaced with several steel bars welded longitudinal enough to protect against flying debris and prevent big bug feet and mandibles from reaching in and snatching him up.

He hopped in, turned the key and the machine let out with a roar as exhaust erupted from the pipes fill the air with a dark cloud.

He shifted, put the truck in gear and the machine charged out of the shed toward the battle ground.

This was by far the biggest moment yet. First time he'd seen so many giant beetles all in one place.

Dealing with the ants was no picnic either but with a large healthy dose of pyrethrin they were eradicated. At least with the ants he was able to locate their nest before they really took off.

Looks like he's behind the eight ball with the beetles.

Beetle heads rose high above the trees and mandibles were popping up everywhere. Trees and debris fell as the mandibles chopped away. But the truck was equipped for this as he managed to dodge the half-cut trees that were falling all around him.

An Army National Guard chopper arrived circling the area. A beetle mandible rose high, and Bob watched it snatch the chopper out of the air like it was nothing but a toy.

The chopper's blades rotating, sparks flying when they hit the beetle's shell causing the steel blades to fall off in chunks.

A large piece whizzed past Bob but not without leaving a little scratch along his left cheek.

Great, as if nothing else can go wrong something has to try and take off my head. I can't afford to lose any more body parts. Running out as it is.

A loud hiss came out of the chopper's exhaust as the mandibles crushed it. The two pilots managed to jump to their death.

Bob pressed the accelerator as he charged toward the beetle all the while weaving between the trees and falling limbs and debris.

"You are dead meat," Bob yelled at the beetle.

He pressed the trigger releasing several rounds hitting the beetle, but the bullets did nothing more than bounce off its shell.

To his left another beetle appeared followed by another. At least twenty of these things surrounded him.

All of them screeching and roaring.

He switched off from the 50 cal and switched over to the flame thrower that he rigged to shoot well over two hundred yards. This he managed to do with the help of his best friend, David, a Hull Technician he'd served on the ship with. When it came to building, David was a master. He could take an old engine and build incredible things with it.

Like that time David got the gas turbines up and running after they'd decided to shut down for whatever reasons that engines do so, they could get through their training ops.

He drove closer toward the beetles. Flame thrower at the ready but he had to get closer.

A man dressed in a suit holding a briefcase was frantically running toward Bob trying to get away from a beetle, but Bob couldn't maneuver his machine quick enough and smacked into the poor ole dude.

Parts of his skin now a preferment fixture on the bars of his machine.

"You stupid idiot!" Bob yelled.

Closer now, Bob pushed the button on the machine igniting it. A flame shot out and engulfed the beetle in fire.

The beetle rose and screeched as the flames burned through its shell. Grey ashes fell like snow.

Bob turned the machine and fired at another beetle. "Burn baby burn," Bob said as he went from one beetle to the next sending each one up in flames.

The smell flesh and bugs wafted in the air, but for each one he was taking down another arrived in its place.

It seemed there was no end.

The stump on his severed leg hurt and ached severely as it always did when he tried to do too much.

He worked through it. Told himself it's all a matter of head over body.

Well, sometimes the body wins.

He sent flame after flame at the pack of beetles in front of him. He thought he was going to get some help when another chopper arrived and shot a missile at the beetles.

The missile exploded igniting the pack of beetles, but the ground shook and rolled as if he were in the ocean causing his machine to rise in the air and flip with enough force to propel Bob several feet in the air.

He landed on his back.

Gasping for air. Eyes wide staring at the pack of beetles in front of him. Lying there he recalled several times where he had a hard time killing roaches in restaurants he'd been servicing and often wondered if there was ever an end to them.

Sometimes the bugs just don't die.

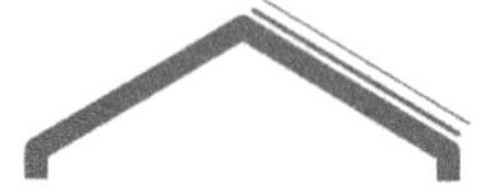

THE DAVEY JONES LOCKER

S N. Ryan scanned the horizon through foggy binocular lenses at approximately 0200 when he heard it.

They were somewhere off the coast of Ireland in the Celtic Sea. He lost track how far away they were.

They had spent the previous night at the festival where they all had overindulged in food and drink. Mostly drink. And those Irish can ever drink. He'd lost track of how many beers he drank. It also wasn't helping that the woman he'd had a good time with gave him the crock itches. He was going to have to see doc about it. He knew what it was. If he was right, this would make the second time he got this.

It was always from the fat women. He didn't know what it was that caused him to end up with a fat chick every time he got drunk. He sure wished he could solve this problem.

Such as another sea adventure for Ryan.

He scratched his itchies as he continued to scan the horizon. He still felt too drunk to really be paying that much attention.

It's okay. Nothing much is going to happen out here anyway.

He was tired and his feet ached from standing so long.

Heeeeelllllo.

One hand on the rail, the other trying to steady the binos as the ship pitched and rolled. This was his first time on a small ship. FFG 19 U.S.S. John A. Moore. Just coming from a carrier, a small ship like this Fast Guided Frigate was a completely different experience.

It was raining and foggy, visibility five miles at most.

He scanned the surface in the direction of the voice, but it was hard to tell which side of the ship the voice was coming from. It sounded deep and guttural.

But really? Surely, it must've only been the wind. It wasn't uncommon to experience strange sounds out here at sea when you're by yourself in the middle of the night. He chalked it off to his imagination getting the best of him. It was still a good idea to follow up with the bridge.

"Bridge. Forward lookout."

"Bridge, aye." It was BM2 Reynolds from East L.A. He could recognize that voice anywhere.

"Did you say something?"

"No."

"I thought I heard a voice."

"All quiet here. Maybe it's the ghosts."

He heard Reynolds chuckle. Reynolds was also known to tell ghost stories when they are alone on watch.

"Heeeellllo. You there. On your port quarter."

It was the same guttural voice. He wiped the lenses with on his jacket and gave another look.

A man waved from a small boat, most likely once used as a lifeboat. What was this sailor doing out here in the middle of the Atlantic on such a small craft?

Was he a fisherman? Did his boat sink.

"You up there. Can yooooooooooou hear me?"

Ryan waved. "I can hear you."

Ryan could tell the sailor's clothes were torn and appeared to be wearing clothes that are far been outdated. His boat was made of wood, no sails, oars or any other means of propulsion. The sailor in the boat bobbed up and down in the seas like a cork. Every time he bobbed down Ryan lost him and when he bobbed back up it was in a different spot. On the side of the boat was written, Elle Adhamh, obviously this was some sort of lifeboat

"Are you shipwrecked. Do you need help?" Ryan asked.

For being out at sea for what appeared to be a while on such a small boat, the sailor seemed to be in great condition.

"It's heeeeeeere. This thing.is...." He waved his arms as if telling them to turn around.

His voice sounded in a state of panic. Ryan was trying to figure out what he was talking about.

"What thing?"

"Ohhh,God. Ohhhh "

Ryan saw the boat lurch backward. Large tentacles wrapped around the boat like long thick veinous fingers reaching up out of the sea. They were dark and covered with suction cups that moved back and forth. They were as large as trees and as thick as their trunks. The sea erupted as the creature surfaced, showering their ship with white foamy water.

My God, he had never seen anything like this in all his life. He never even knew something like this existed.

Ryan heard the wood boat cracking and crunching under the thing's fingers.

Boat splinters and debris erupted. The man screamed and all was gone.

The long tentacles clawed at the waves as they inched their way toward their ship.

One of the things tentacles smacked Ryan in the chest knocking him against the bulkhead.

Ryan gasped, grasped his chest as he caught his breath.

Looking at those things. Those tentacles.

Watching as they climbed up the side of the ship. Their suctions cups opening and closing like hundreds of tiny mouths.

He reached to press the button on his sound powered phone but they were gone.

The tentacles must've knocked them off when they smacked him.

There is no way we're getting out of this one, he thought.

This is going to be it.

He stayed as low to the deck as he possibly could as a tentacle swiped across the bridge above him.

He heard the steel crushing. Squeaking, cracking as the tentacle smacked it as if it were nothing more than a tin can.

Reynolds and the Officer of the deck soared through the air and landed in the water.

He had to admit, he wasn't exactly disappointed to see the officer if the deck, Lt House ,screaming and flopping around in the water.

He hated Lt. House and House hated him. Mostly because Ryan wouldn't do everything he said and always argued back.

Now there was no more Lt. House.

No saving him either. Not that he would really try that hard.

He saw Reynolds waving his arms but there was no saving him as a tentacle wrapped around Reynolds crushing him.

While those tentacles were busy crushing the life out of Reynolds, Ryan saw the other tentacles climbing up the side of the ship wrapping themselves around the stern.

We're doomed. Ryan thought. He felt there was no way to get out of this one. To think on one of his other ships he survived a werewolf attack.

Now this.

Go figure.

Honestly, he couldn't even say he saved the ship from the werewolf attack but he did manage to avoid being captured, unlike his shipmate, Baron, which he'd heard was captured and brought on board their ship.

It was a miracle Ryan was still alive.

Being in the Navy proved to be more adventurous than he cared for. Now, all he wanted to do was make it home and get to his family.

Oh, and tell his grandpa the Navy wasn't for him.

The Army's commercial, 'BE ALL YOU CAN BE,' came to his mind. Of course, being in the army wasn't any better.

A tentacle swept across the mast knocking it off, tearing it and taking a large part of the deck off with it.

These things were able to bend and shred steel as if were nothing but a tiny toothpick.

Their ship was nothing more than a tiny toy floating around in its very own bathtub.

The creature rose as if it were climbing the swells and was larger than Earth as if it were the coming of Jesus Christ. Suction cups all over its body. Tentacles covered its face like a beard, so large and so close he could see tiny bits of ships and bones.

He saw a bow of what looked like a small fishing boat called the S.S. MINOW.

No way, he thought. Absolutely no way.

Am I going to be like that? Am I going to be lost out here and end up alone on a deserted island?

At this point any place would be better than out here.

The creature's head grew larger and larger like a dark story cloud.

It's eyes looking at him.

Ryan moved toward the ladder down to the deck bellow. He had to get away from up here and get lower where it would be harder for the creature to see and so its tentacles couldn't find him.

He could feel the ship listing hard to port as he climbed down the ladder which he was basically climbing sideways at this point.

The railing was wet and covered with salt as he lost his grip and fell to the deck below hitting his head on the capstan.

His head throbbed and ached. His whole body ached.

The ship lurched with a sudden jerk as Ryan could clearly see now they were high in the air.

Tentacles wrapped around the mid-section and the stern..

Sliding across the deck he managed to grab hold of the fire hose from the station and wrapped his arms around it. His clothes were soaked and heavy. His eyes burned from the saltwater splashing in his face.

The creature smelled of musty mildew coupled with a rotten fish odor sort of like tuna fish sitting in the hot sun.

He wanted desperately to get away from this thing.

He held on as he felt the ship coming down and slammed onto the sea. The creature bouncing the ship around like a little boy playing with a small boat in the bathtub.

This was a good time to pray.

But what good would praying do? It was clear that God must hate him.

Amidst all the commotion, he could hear the voice of his mother in his head telling him that he wasn't going to like it in the Navy and that he should stay home in Indiana and get a good job at the factory.

He didn't consider himself a factory worker. He longed for excitement. Adventure.

'Well, you sure got it,' he could hear his mother say in her Kentucky twang.

He wanted some fried chicken and mashed taters sounded pretty good right about now.

If he survives this, he could hear his mother saying how she had told him so. She never did like any of the decisions he made.

He grabbed the fire axe from the rack and started hacking away at the tentacle that was wrapped around the ship.

He breathed and pulsated as if it had its own life. The suction cups opening and closing.

The tentacle moved toward him as if it could sense where he was. It was as if the suction cups were hungry for human flesh.

He hacked away at it.

The blade digging deep into the tentacle making it squirm around like a worm. The more he hacked the madder the thing became and the tentacle thrashed and squirmed around more.

Slamming onto the deck, ripping away the weather deck rail. Another tentacle whipped around, grabbed the capstan and ripped it off the deck flinging it out to sea.

This thing was something more than just a giant octopus.

He remembered the Kraken. He'd heard all the myths, the stories. But this thing was much larger than the Kraken.

This thing was real.

Vicious.

He hacked and hacked away at the tentacle. The skin felt like he was chopping into eight inches of thick leather with the way the axe bounced off with each blow. At least he managed to leave a large gash with each slash.

It was as if the other tentacle could feel the pain as it rose high and slammed onto the ship.

The creature let out an ear-piercing scream.

He knew he only baely put a dent in the thing. He was going to have to do something more if he was going to kill it and had any chance of surviving.

He was going to survive. He was a Boatswain Mate. Boatswain Mates are the backbone of the ship and are tough as leather.

Nowhere in the Blue Jackets Manuel did it say anything about fighting sea monsters.

The creature's head popped to the surface. Glaring at him with its slitted eyes.

Strange how a creature so large could have such small eyes. Eyes the size of a human as if it wanted to see who the wise guy was chopping away at his tentacle.

It had something in its mouth.

What is that?

He could see feet dangling.

Blood spurted as the creature chewed vigorously. Like an Italian eating calamari. His shipmate's blood squirting on him.

He hacked and hacked as hard as he could. All he seemed to do was only manage to leave a few gashes. Sure, the creature was feeling it, but it wasn't doing anything to slow it down.

The ship finally steadied even though she was now leaning on her port side and taking on water from the bellow decks. So, trying to get down to the ladder was impossible.

He could hear the cries of his shipmates as they've been tossed into the sea and scattered about.

There was no chance of even getting a life raft.

His best bet was to stay here.

He was going to have to continue to fight it and hope for the best.

Once again, he could hear his mother's words, 'I told you not to do this,' in his mind.

He grabbed his head and cursed his mother's words out of his mind.

Another tentacle had another one of his shipmates. It was the Chief Boats form New Jersey. He was cursing at thing all the way up till the creature shoved him in his mouth.

No more Chief Boats.

He and the Chief had spent a lot of party time together as the Chief gave him some of that, what sailors call, at the bar extra instruction.

Ryan crawled around the edge of the deck making his way into a little alcove where the mooring lines were stowed.

He caught his breath as he thought about his next move. He was really praying for this creature to go away but that didn't look like it was happening.

He seemed safe here for now.

But the ship continued to take on more water. From where he was sitting, he could see half the ship was gone. From mid-section to stern.

The water sounded like he was standing under Niagara Falls as it took on water and sinking quickly.

There was the pop pop popping sound of the ship's rivets being ripped out followed by creaking and groaning as he watched the other half of the ship sink.

It was only a matter of time before he was to go down. He could feel her listing more and more.

The creature's tentacles wrapped fingers around on the deck as if they were searching for him. He didn't know too much about it but it was like its tentacles had sensors.

The creature's head surfaced again. Its eye staring at him.

A boat hook hung on the bulkhead to his left. He grabbed it and yelled for the creature, calling it every kind of name he could of.

I've had it with this thing, he said to himself as he rammed the pointed end of the boat hook into the creature's eye.

It screeched. Blood oozed out from between the point of the boat hook and its eye.

Tentacles thrashed about wildly, smacking the boat. Bending steel and tearing off the rest of the railing.

He grabbed hold of the ship and wrapped its tentacles around it for what seemed completely around.

It was sinking the boat.

The tentacles pushed the boat down deep into the ocean.

Ryan didn't know what to do.

What can I do? He thought.

Water rushed over the gunwale as the boat was being pushed deeper and deeper.

Ryan had no other place to climb other than to crawl up as high as he could on the pile of mooring lines but it was only going to be a matter of time before he met his demise and was going to go down with the ship.

He saw an emergency box in the angle iron.

Great.

There we go. That's something.

His fingers felt numb and his hands were shaking as the cold was now starting to set in.

His whole body shivered.

He opened the box and grabbed the flare gun.

He felt something wrap around his leg. It was a tentacle. In one quick swoop he was yanked into the air being waved around.

He was yanked to the left.

To the right.

He went into the water and back up again. Salt water filled his mouth and his lungs as he coughed out as much as he could..

Bam bam bam

His body slamming o on top of the sea felt like concrete.

A sharp burst of pain shot through his leg and up his back. He heard a crack in his right leg as he smacked into the water again and again.

Right now he just wanted this whole thing to be over. He wished for the creature to just go ahead and eat him and get this over with.

Then he noticed that somehow through all that getting banged around he managed to hold onto the flare gun.

When the tentacle brough him high in the air it gave him a good view of the creature's head.

It was hard trying to get a good shot at it with the way he kept getting thrashed around made it hard to get in a steady shot. He only had one chance to get this right. If he blew it then most likely he would be down the creature's gut as a mid-night snack.

This was like a ride gone bad at an amusement park. He'd heard about those situations where roller coaster cars got derailed and flew off the track. Then he remembered about reading one situation where a young kid fell out of the seat of one of those sky diving rides with the huge tower.

There was nothing anybody could ever prepare for this. Even the Navy hadn't trained about what a crew should do if attacked by a sea monster. They were good at running drills for everything else.

As he was being whipped around, he grasped the gun so tight his hands were numb. But he kept telling himself not to let go of it. No matter what.

The tentacle brought him around and steadied for a split second.

That's all I need.

Stay right there.

"Don't you dare move," he said as if the creature was going to actually listen.

He fired the flare gun straight at it and shot a big burning hole in the creature's face.

It thrashed and groaned and screeched.

The tentacle released its grasp and Ryan fell into the sea.

"How you doing there, Lad?"

Ryan heard a raspy, gruff voice in that same Irish accent. He could hear it but it took him a minute to open his eyes. He felt something hard and cold against his back. He felt wet and was shivering. He could tell he was on a boat.

But how?

The last thing he remembered was shooting the creature and falling into the sea.

Ryan coughed as he tried to catch his breath. His vision was blurry, but he could tell he was on some kind of small boat and a man with a heavy beard and whiskey on his breath staring at him. "Where am I?"

"You're on my boat, Lad. Took a bit of a spill too. You're safe here."

"Who are you?" He tried to sit up but the man guided him back down.

"You just lie down there. Rest. You're okay here."

Ryan's vision was beginning to come in and he could see the man more clearly now. "I remember you. You're that fisherman in that small boat."

"Aye. You are right, Lad. You shot that creature down. He'll be back though. I promise you that."

"What do you mean?"

"That thing has been terrorizing the coast of Ireland for centuries. Sunk my boat as well. Sent me to the Davy Jones Locker. Almost sent you there too. Good thing I saw you out here."

"Who?"

"The Davey Jones Locker where all the drowned sailors from sunken vessels go.

Ryan's body finally succumbed to the bitter cold and rain as he fell asleep. When he woke he was lying in the hospital bed. By the looks of the scenery outside and hearing the voices of the nurses he could tell he was back in Ireland.

"Ahh, you're awake," the nurse said.

He loved her rich accent. She was tall, pretty and had long black hair. She was perhaps the most beautiful woman he'd ever saw.

"Am I....?"

"You're in Ireland, lad. You're an American. Yes?"

"Yes."

"You're ship sunk at sea. Took a good hit on the ole noggin you did. An old fisherman found you and brought you back."

It took him a moment to recall the events as they slowly unfolded in his mind. Then he remembered.

"That Captain. Was it that Captain?"

"I'm not sure. Just some old fisherman. Didn't give his name."

"His boat's name was the Ellie Adhamh. I remember seeing that. I must find him and thank him."

She guided him back down as he tried to sit up. "You just rest for now. I think you are mistaken though."

"Mistaken?"

"Yes. The name of the boat you mention sunk a long time ago, several years to be exact. The whole crew went down with the boat. Story is it supposedly was attacked by a giant sea monster. But with you being a sailor yourself, I'm sure you know about those sailor tales."

ATTACK OF THE GIANT SPIDERS

It wasn't bad enough that Clark had to battle with the giant beetle let alone having seen a giant spider walking through the demolished development. It was only three days later.

Here we go again, he thought. Just like a bad car. The trouble just keeps on coming.

Jeeez. It never ends.

Isn't enough, enough already?

Heck, dude. He told himself. The party is just getting started.

He wouldn't have believed it if he hadn't seen it for himself. The thing was massive in size as it towered over everything. He saw it walking over the houses as if it were heading out to a field somewhere.

What is up with all these giant creatures?

What happened that caused all this?

Probably, another one of them secret government experiments gone bad. It's always the government. As if the pandemic they started wasn't bad enough already.

He knew there was no way he could be the last man on Earth. There had to be others that survived. He just hadn't found them yet.

Others were out here somewhere.

He looked at the picture of his wife and son he kept folded in his wallet. He had them on his cell phone but those were useless now. It lasted for as long as the battery lasted and with there being no way to get electricity, they were useless along with all the other electronic devices that these corporations thought they were going to make the world a better place.

His wife and son had to be out here somewhere. He prayed every night that he would find them.

HA HA.

Jokes on them.

He chuckled at his thought.

At some point he was going to have to get some ammo. He should be able to stock up in town. The place may be in ruins, but he knew somewhat of his whereabouts. He knew he was in an area they called Beach Grove. He didn't live far from here and grew up a mile down the street.

Before the attack on Earth, the beach Grove area was quickly becoming the laughingstock of the nation. With toothless fat people fighting over scooters.

Good thing there are no more electronics.

He shouldered his rifle as he made his way down the hill toward town where he would find a gun shop. One thing about Indiana is that there are plenty of gun shops and plenty of survivalists. Some had bunkers made going all the way back in the day when his grandparents talked about a nuclear war threat from Russia.

To his right down the street he saw the old pest control building he used to work at. He couldn't help but chuckle at this one at the irony. A pest control building demolished by giant bugs.

Their company trucks flipped upside down.

Yeah, looked like the bugs were really intimidated.

Suppose there was no stopping that one. To think their termite inspection renewal notices went out last week.

How funny.

He thought he better stop talking to himself like this or he was going to go crazy. Not that it really mattered. Nobody was around anyway.

Once he made his way down what was once Main Street he stocked up on some canned food at the local grocery, some jerky and grabbed a handful of snickers bars. The store used to be a Wal-Mart so there was going to be plenty.

He kicked over a pile of debris as he made his way down an aisle. Surveillance cameras and wires were all strewn about.

He saw arms and legs sticking out from under a pile of books and shelves. He kicked over the rubbage and saw a man with a tag. STORE MANAGER.

The thought crossed his mind that maybe his wife and son were in here somewhere, but it wasn't likely. She stopped coming to this store once those idiots got into a fight over a scooter and created all sorts of disturbance in the shampoo aisle. The store had been having other problems in the past, so it got to the point it wasn't worth coming in.

Until now.

Once loaded up he made his way back out into the jungle.

An explosion down the hill got his attention as a mushroom ball of fire erupted. He something that looked shiny and silky like and as he got closer he saw it was spider webbing.

The webbing was thick like half inch sized rope.

Was it even possible for spiders to create something this large?

It is if they're tall as the sky.

He saw pick up trucks stuck in the webbing with their tires still rotating. Seme trailers and he even saw a Peterbilt. It was as if whatever came in here became instantly trapped in its webbing.

He had no idea how he was going to get around something like this. More webbing was strewn from demolished building to demolished building each part of a web interconnecting with another forming a large impenetrable large wall.

He saw everything you could possibly think of stuck in this webbing.

He saw ants the size of houses with their feet still kicking just waiting for the spider to come along for whenever it decides it wants a meal.

House flies the size of semi-trucks.

Of course, there were a few humans in the web as well. One of them he recognized as, Roy, his old branch manager he never got along with.

How funny, he thought. And this knucklehead thought he had all the answers on how to control insects.

Suppose nobody prepared him for this one.

At first, he wasn't sure what made this area so bad. The more he looked around and thought about it, it all made sense.

A large sun beam glowed through this area, reflecting off the building windows making everything all glistening and bright.

Of course, now it made perfect sense.

The spiders are going to build their webs into the light so when other insects fly toward the light they get stuck in the web. Humans and everything else just seemed to get in their way.

This was their world now.

Their big bug world.

Never in his day did he think that there would come a time when the world was attacked by giant insects. There was no way these things could even be from here.

Here, he thought the new so-called president was going send them to World War three with Russian.

Looks like we had other problems they failed to mention.

It didn't matter how many times he scratched his head over the whole matter, it still wasn't changing the fact that humans were now an extinct species and now the bugs ruled.

Unless something else comes along. Like maybe actual aliens perhaps. Which from the way things have been going it wouldn't surprise him in the least.

He saw smoke and fire popping up everywhere. The streets he knew are all now quiet, desolate and beyond repair.

No more people walking the streets even though a lot of them on this side of town were up to no good.

No more cars and traffic.

Somehow in the blink of an eye the world changed in a flash.

He continued calling for his wife and son hoping they would hear his voice. He thought back as to what they could've possible been doing that day. Most likely they wouldn't be in this area.

His mind was blank and he found it hard to focus considering all that had been happening. Having the world blow up right in front of your face tends to send your mind off course.

How long ago did this happen? He thought back to the whole beetle incident and realized it had to be at least a couple months since that.

It was baseball. He remembered she needed to take him to get a new baseball bat because he was starting high school next year.

They would be at the Dicks or Play it Again Sports.

Both of those were in Greenwood. So, yes, there was that possibility they would be in that area. He could only hope and pray they would be alive. They had to be there. The problem was the stores were at least eight miles from where he was and trying to hump around all this garbage was one thing, this giant webbing was another.

He found the webbing amazing beyond belief. Fascinating, as it was as large as mooring lines. Run into that at night, there would be no getting out of it.

He couldn't take his eyes off Roy stuck in the webbing. Even though he couldn't help but find it amusing on how he was still in his Orkin uniform.

Things that make you go HMMMM.

To make it even more humorous an Orkin truck was stuck way on top of the webbing that reach higher than any tree could ever reach. He couldn't help but wonder how it got way up there.

Out of nowhere came a loud scream as somebody jumped on his back and knocked him the ground. Arms wrapped around his neck and legs as whoever this was wrestled him to the ground. He was shocked. Confused about what was going on. It had been several days since he'd seen anybody other than large bugs and now somebody out of nowhere jumps on his back.

They wrestled and entwined on the ground. Punching at each other in the ribs. The attacker didn't seem like a large man and obviously didn't have any training at least not enough compared to his Marine Corps training, so he didn't find it hard to apprehend him and had his attacker on his back in no time.

The attacker's clothes were tattered, blue jeans and a black T-Shirt which read, SARCASTIC SOCIETY.

Things just keep getting even more humorous, he thought.

The attacker swung but Clark grabbed his hands and pinned them. "Settle down. I don't want to hurt you."

Clark knew this guy was trying to rob him of his M-16 and ammo. It would only make sense considering Earth was on its last stretch so any survivors were going to do what they had to do in order to stay alive at least for as long as they could.

This guy was nervous about something and obviously afraid. Clark had seen that kind of fear in many eyes in his day. Part of him was glad there were others, it meant there was still hope. The other part of him was afraid. This meant there were going to be more vicious groups out here.

"It's after me! That thing."

"What thing?"

"It's giant. Unbelievable."

"What is it?"

Once Clark felt the guy was calmed down enough and posed no threat, he let him up so he could explain himself. "There are giant bugs out here. I mean huge."

"You don't have to tell me that. I've had a run in with several."

Clark gave the man a sip of water as he was still trying to catch his breath. He went on explaining to Clark how the bugs destroyed his house and ate his family. Clark saw his eyes widen as the fella pointed at something behind him.

"Like that," he said.

The thing towered over them and was tall as the clouds. Clark's first thought was that there was no way this was happening. No way. It wasn't humanly possible for insects to get this large. First his run in with the giant beetle and now this. Just when you thought you've seen enough of the world and it has nothing left to offer and he thought about how relieved he was when he managed to make it out of the Marine Corps alive you can bet something else will come along and disrupt and change turn your world upside down.

Clark was about ready to say he knew there were spiders out here because of the webs but the poor fella beat him to it and yelled. "Spider!"

The spider towered over them and was so close Clark could see the reflection in its eyes. All eight of them. Its body was hairy, and he could see the large red hour glass shape on its abdomen which only meant one thing, Black Widow.

"isn't that just our luck," Clark said.

"Why you say it like that?" he asked sensing the nervousness in Clark's voice.

"That's a Black Widow."

"Dude. You kidding me?"

"Wish I were."

A black widow that large had enough venom to wipe out an entire earth population. Clark knew that it wasn't likely the widow was going to bite them. She was more apt to save her venom for a more serous prey when she needed to eat and it was going to take her a while for her venom to replenish. A widow that size it would take at least a minimum of three days. The real question was how long has it been since she'd bitten anything? It really didn't matter because he was going to blow the thing away and be done with it.

The attacker said he wasn't going to stick around to see what happened and turned and ran. Clark tried to grab him before but his pant leg cuff just brushed his fingers. Clark barely got the words out for him to stop but not before the poor fella ran smack into the web. Screaming, his arms and legs waving on the web. Clark knew there was no way to get him off that.

Clark removed his hunting knife from its sheave and sliced at the webbing. The strands were sticking and was like cutting into a glue as his knife stuck. He took little slices and cuts, all the while the attacker screaming for Clark to get him off of here. Which he really didn't want to do in the first place considering the guy was trying to sneak up on him and kill him and now he is rescuing him and he wouldn't have if the guy hadn't proven to be incompetent and just nervous and afraid. A typical civilian with lack of training.

The pile of trash and debris erupted from under the web as a tree like leg reached up from underneath all the rubble and grabbed the screaming attacker pulling him down into its nesting area. Clark heard crunching and chomping as the guy let out with ear-piercing screams before all went silent.

Clark didn't see it coming when he felt himself lifting high into the air. The hair on its leg were like needles as they poked through his chest and his legs. To Clark they were like over-sized porcupine needles. He could barely move. The spider's leg was like hugging a tree in the Red Forrest.

He grabbed hold of one of the hairs and hung as he dangled at around a hundred feet. He was able to look down and see everything all around as that time he was a kid when he climbed to the top of the fire tower.

Clark jolted and swung as he held on with all his might as the spider moved further down the path. Everything was covered with more webbing making the place look like the aftermath of an apocalypse.

This looked like their nesting area. It was just his luck that he would end up in the nesting area of the Black Widow.

Holding on with one hand he managed to lock his fingers into a gab in the spider's legs as he had done when he was climbing rocks in Colorado. The spider's leg was as hard as rock mountain. He reached around to his right-side hip and grabbed the knife from the sheave.

His fingers sweat and hurt as they slipped on the cliff area from the leg until he was barely holding on from his fingertips. Pain shot through his arm and all the way down his leg. He could feel the muscles in his arms stretching and pulling as if something was inside twisting him like a pretzel.

Cutting at the leg was like trying to cut through a tree trunk with a steak knife. Little chunks of thick bark like skin flew off but he was barely able to make a decent enough cut. Whatever he was doing was affecting the spider as Clark suddenly found himself being swooped even higher. Up and down up and down he went as if on a wild ride at the amusement park. With all the bad timing and in a strange way all the motion made him think of that spider ride at the park except a thousand times faster and a couple hundred feet higher.

His fingers slipping, he was forced to drop the knife and grab hold and managed to wrap his legs around the leg providing more bracing.

He had no idea what he was going to do now. The only thing he felt he could do was hold on and ride it out and hope for the best he bobbed up and down. A loud explosion sounded each time the spider's foot touched the ground and leaving large craters in its wake.

BOOM... BOOM...BOOM...

Clouds of dirt debris flew in his face and felt like sand in his eyes making them sting and hurt. Chunks the size of boulders flew up from the spider's foot. Every time the spider's leg came up he was able to twist around on the leg to get a better grip and was able to see where she was heading. There was nothing but webs and a large pit the size of a lake. It was then he realized she was taking him to her nest.

He almost forgot about the three grenades he had in the pouch he'd grabbed from a closet at an Army Surplus store he was in the other day.

"That's it girl. Take me to your nest," he said aloud. "Let's go home. I'll have a nice little surprise waiting for ya when we get there."

He wondered if the spider even knew he was still there. She stopped walking long enough for him to climb higher up her leg. Lord, this was high. A couple hundred feet at least. A few times he almost lost his footing and nearly slipped off but managed to grab hold of one of her hairs and held on. It was like looking down at from the New York skyscraper. He was high enough he could see the nest inside the pit, and it was covered in hundreds of tiny spiders that just hatched from their eggs.

This whole thing could've been an even bigger disaster. As if this wasn't a big enough disaster already. Looking for a nest this size would've taken him days to get here and most likely he wouldn't have made it. The spider had made such quick large strides he had no idea where he was. What he did know was that he was miles and miles away from where he'd first started when he encountered the beast.

He grabbed a grenade from the pouch and held it tight. Waiting for the spider to get closer.

A little closer.

Then for some unknown reason she decided to turn around. If he was going to do this, he was going to have to do this now. He pulled the pin on the grenade, squeezed the trigger and tossed it in the hole.

BOOM

Spiders and dirt erupted in a cloudy mixture. Startled by the sudden blast, the spider rose high, squealed, which caught his attention because he'd never known spiders to squeal but this one sure enough did.

Ticked off that somebody just blew up her babies the spider took off through the jungle of housing debris. Clark was doing all he could do to hold on and wasn't sure how much longer he could keep this up.

He grabbed another grenade from his pouch, pulled the pin, squeezed the trigger and wedged it in tight between the spider's hairs and slid down the leg as fast as he could and jumped off.

He tumbled down the hill head over head. Hitting branches and boards. He felt he'd banged his head a couple times on a rock or something before coming to rest at the bottom of the hill just in time...

He watched as spider guts and flesh blew in a mushroom cloud explosion. The spider screeched and groaned as her remains quickly disintegrated into nothing but embers and ash.

Well now, Clark thought as he rubbed his head. That sure was quite a ride. Who would've thought that exterminating bugs would get to this level?

He stood up, brushed himself off and with nothing else on his back he climbed back up the small hill in search for the next town where he could reload on his ammo and hopefully get some new guns. Lord knows he was going to need it. Somewhere, out here he knew his wife and son are waiting for him.

THE CANNIBALS OF MYSTERY ISLAND

"There on the shelf is what is believed to be John's scull. It was found some maybe ten years later floating off the coast of Bermuda on the very boat we're sitting in now. Found by yours truly. She may be an old gal, but she is just as seaworthy today as when she first set sail. Couldn't imagine sailing with anyone else."

"Wasn't it just a myth? Really, an invisible island?"

"Ahh, my friend. Not just invisible. It disappears and doesn't reappear for another year. When it does appear it is only eight to ten hours at the most."

"I'd have to see that to believe it." He sits back in his chair and lights a cigar.

"And those two spears you see on the wall were from the cannibals found by my fisherman friend. He finds things out there every once in a while, and brings them back to me."

"In fact, the chair you're sitting on was where, Rachel, his finance at the time died. A fisherman who was very familiar with the area and the island itself went on a search after he heard where they were going and said that it was a bad time and something bad was going to happen. He kept an eye on them so to speak.

Good thing he knew where to look, or he wouldn't have found her if he hadn't. She managed to stay alive long enough tell her story. God rest her soul.

If you look closely, you can see that little crack there where it appears to have been done by a spear from the cannibals. People tried to tell him it wasn't a good time to go because the island and its cannibals were due to appear any day. It was getting close to that time, you know. Unfortunately, he never believed in it. Seriously, who in their right state of mind would ever believe in an invisible island of cannibals, especially in these days? Suppose no one can blame him.

As far as we know, no one made it off that island alive. Fascinating how Rachel managed to do it. She was living proof that we were right about the island all along."

He puffed his cigar and blew three smoke rings. "And you say this woman managed to escape it?"

"She did. Fascinating."

"How exactly did she die if she were able to tell you all of this?"

"The doctor said it was most likely a heart attack. Fear, he said. A deep dark fear."

This is what she told me happened and how she escaped. God rest her soul "

JOHN HARVARD THOUGHT this was the life. The life he'd always dreamed of. Being out at sea, watching the sun rise this early morning as they left their Florida home on their way to Bermuda.

He breathed in deeply and exhaled as he found the salty air refreshing and rewarding. He had one major fault that cost him. He was not a hard worker. One of those that always looked for the easy way of life and in no way was he prepared for work that entails being out at sea.

The wind was a little rough that day and not that we knew this but that was our first warning that a bad storm was on its way.

The swells were only about five foot as seagulls circled above as they escorted them out of the gate and into the breakwater.

People waved to us as we headed down the channel and we waved at the light house just before entering the break water. A few college kids out on spring break were starting their party early passed us by on a nice Bertram Yacht.

I was lying on the bow sunbathing, enjoying life as if all was right and perfect in the world but I wasn't the one that knew what I was doing. John was the one in charge and liked to be called the captain. It was a game he liked to play. I guess it made him feel like he was in charge. By the way he was smiling and looking out at the water and watching his sails I knew he was in his happy place.

This was every man's dream.

His dream. Which I didn't mind. At first, I wasn't so thrilled with the idea of being so far out here, but it was so relaxing. It felt good to leave everything behind even if it was for a short time.

Wow was it nice getting away from the office. A break from the corporate world. He hated being in business and often thought he should've just taken up a trade instead of following in his father's footsteps and being a lawyer, which was way overrated.

As for as that moment, that life was behind him. More than he realized. For the next two weeks he could pretend to be someone else.

Now, Lady Luck was on her way to Bermuda.

Except, Lady wasn't so lady like or lucky like during the three-day storm we encountered. He was told we were heading out at the wrong time with it being hurricane season, but John Harvard wasn't the type of man to take advice from anyone except himself. He said you can't let those old fogies tell you what to do.

Some would say he was a fool, and some would say that he was living life large. Too large as was our case. Larger than I care for, that's for sure.

The Lady's Luck's hull was glossy white with her name written in large black fancy letters across the bow. Her rails were mahogany wood that he'd spent hours wiping down and required continuous touch up.

The clouds were dark and had dangerous written all over them and they were approaching quickly.

That was our warning.

When we started out there wasn't a cloud in the sky, but wow did it ever change quickly.

I stayed below tucked away trying my best to ride out the storm while. My tummy wasn't doing so well. Too much up and down motion. It was a weird feeling. Nothing like I've ever felt before. All I could do was trust my husband's sailing abilities and be confident he would get them through this.

In my case I was a little too trusting because the first words out of my mouth were, 'I think we may want to postpone our trip and do this another day like people are suggesting.'

"Nonsense," he said. "We cannot allow the weather to control our lives."

So, we set out to begin our wrestle with Mother Nature herself.

During the storm the antenna was ripped off, lost auxiliary power and the sail was torn and taken away. He thought he was smart because he was prepared for that very situation, one can never be too careful, that was until the mast bent like a pretzel.

I would peek my head out of the hatch and ask how everything was going. His reply was as would be expected from such a man. "We're doing just fine. Gonna ride us out of this in not time. Not to worry. Not to worry."

The fact that he repeated, not to worry, twice made me even more concerned. At that moment I was thinking that I should've put my foot down and demanded we wait for better weather.

He'd read countless books on how sailors handled such storms and had read about sailors that tackled Cape Horn. But deep down he couldn't see how anyone could prepare for something like this.

The waves were towering. A wave so massive in size and powerful beyond belief. He gripped the helm for dear life as the waves crashed over

Lady Luck as if they were intentionally washing away every bit of luck out of her.

He screamed at the storm. Cursed the God of the sea though he was too green of a sailor to know that was something you just do not do. I'm not a sailor but even I know better than that.

It was as if Poseidon himself were saying, "Now you done ticked me off. You disrespect me, now you're going to pay the price.

He came to his senses then and decided he'd better get down below. It was a hard crawl back to the hatch as he stayed as low as he possible. At times the waves crashed over us with such force I thought for sure he was going to get washed overboard.

The waves brought the boat to the crest of the wave and had steadied enough for him to open the hatch and get inside just before she took the deep plunged down.

He said we were just going to have to ride out the rest of the storm and hope for the best.

This got my attention. "What do you mean hope for the best?"

"Little rough out there?" He was trying to be careful to not say anything but realized he'd done screwed the keeping calm thing up.

"We're going to be okay, right? "You said you are a sailor and know what you're doing." Honestly, I don't know why I asked that. I knew we were not going to be okay. It something you just know. I felt it even more when he came clean and told me he'd never done this before. What an idiot.

I was calling him every name in the book in my mind. I remembered thinking that if I survive any of this there is no way I'm marrying him.

"Going to be fine. Just a little rain and weather."

The boat shook, rolled hard to port and abruptly to the starboard with such force it tossed me across the room causing me to bang my head on the book shelf book shelf.

I remember feeling the boat rock and saw our cabin fill with water and that was all I remembered of that.

The next thing I knew I woke with my face in the sand.

I HAD SAND IN MY MOUTH and all over my face. No idea where we were except, I knew we were on some beach. I had no idea how long I'd been lying there. All I know was that I was redder than a lobster.

I managed to get up on my feet. Wow, how they hurt so bad. I washed them off in the water allowing my feet to cool. They were so sore.

Palm trees lined the outer part of the beach that looked all sorts of woodsy. I heard birds of various kinds, and I couldn't help but notice two vultures circling around us.

I walked down along the beach when I saw John. I called his name, but he didn't answer.

His clothes were torn, and his back was red. I turned him over. "John. John. Wake up." I could see his chest moving so that was a good thing. At least he was breathing.

I slapped him a couple times while calling his name. Finally, he woke up.

He rubbed his eyes as I helped him sit up. "Where are we?"

"Looks like we're on some kind of island."

"Seriously?"

"Yes. Seriously. I wouldn't joke about something like that."

He looked out into the ocean. "Where's our boat?"

"Gone. My guess is we both passed out and woke up here. At least we're safe, I said. I had to admit, it felt good to be alive. I thought for sure after that bad storm we were in we were going to be lying at the bottom of the sea somewhere, never to be seen or heard from again.

I asked him if he I had any idea where we could be. He said he wasn't aware of any islands in our path and that we must have really drifted off course.

All my life I never thought I'd be stranded on a deserted island. I did like the sound of the waves crashing on the beach. It was very relaxing. So relaxing that if didn't know any better I'd say we were in a resort somewhere after traveler season and we had it all to ourselves.

I assisted John closer to the water and helped him get cleaned up. He tried to stand up and suddenly grabbed his leg and fell back down.

"My leg. My leg!"

"You're bleeding," I said. Narrow rivulets of blood dripped down his leg."

"It hurts so bad."

"It's broke." So broke I could see the bone sticking out. I told him not to look at it because I didn't want him going into shock.

"I don't think you should've taken off your shirt," he said. I had nothing on but my white bra.

"Doesn't matter. Looks like we have the place to ourselves anyway. Makes no difference at this point."

"We don't know for sure we're along. Could be natives."

"Haaa. Natives. I don't think they're around anymore. This isn't 1912. If there's any natives around in 2023, I'd be shocked." I was glad to see at least he was feeling well enough to make jokes.

I had him lay down and I gathered up a piece of wood from the tree line and used it as a splint and tied the shirt around it. It wasn't the best of work but at least it would do until we somehow figure out a way to get off the island.

With it getting dark it was time to settle in and we figured we might as well get some rest. I helped him back to a spot I had picked out along the tree line where we could stay sheltered. It was getting windy, and the air was cooling down. With our clothes as wet as they were to us it felt like freezing.

It got so cold and so dark, we couldn't see anything, not even our hands in front of our faces. We could hear the ocean.

Later we woke to a howling, like coyotes and there were a lot of them.

"I feel like a wounded animal out here," John said.

I prayed that they didn't pick up our scent.

The next morning, John had the idea to make spears to defend ourselves. We sharpened them using rocks. Amazing what you can do when you have to we could take any chances.

John also thought we should start building a raft so we could get out of here. He got the idea from a book he'd been reading.

I went out and collected bamboo while he started on the raft. I don't think he knew what he was doing though because he kept tearing down and rebuilding. There was a lot of huffing and groaning on his part.

It took us three days to build just a simple flat raft. We made a canopy out of palm leaves to protect us from the sun.

John looked at the raft as if he'd just built the greatest project ever. It was crooked and I had my doubts if that thing would stay afloat. John shrugged it off and said that it would work just fine.

Let me see. Take my chances on a lopsided raft in the ocean that looked like it was going to come apart in a couple hours maybe less than that or stay here on land where it was safe.

I chose to stay on land where it was safe and told John. We were in no condition to try and tackle the sea again. I couldn't believe he had the guts, or may it be stupidness, not sure yet, that he was willing to risk trying it again. The way I saw it, we were lucky that we are alive.

Anyway, John was convinced it would work and so he was going to wait till morning and we would set out. To this day, I'm not sure I knew what he was thinking. I sure didn't want to risk it. I made up my mind that I wasn't going and told him that if he were doing it then he was going to have to go at it alone. He agreed and said that once he made it back, he would send help.

I didn't know how he was going to do that either because we had no idea where we were. We've never seen anything like this place.

Turned out, my problem with the raft took care of itself with the help of Mother Nature once again. A bad storm came upon us, a very bad one with heavy gusty winds that lasted for well over a couple hours. We were safe where we were. Still getting wet but we were protected because we were in a lower area. The rain came down heavier than anything I'd ever saw, and it smacked into the raft tearing it up. Not much later the winds blew the raft. We watched it shredding in the air as it was being blown away.

Just like that, the raft was gone.

I HAD TO ADMIT, JOHN still wasn't in any shape to move around much so I went out and did a little exploring for myself just to check out and see what this place was all about. It was beautiful. There were so many different types of trees and I even found a beautiful waterfall. It was at least twenty feet surrounded by rocks and it looked like a cave was behind the water. The perfect place to swim and bathe.

We had another problem. We had no idea what we were going to eat. We knew there were wolves around because we heard them but we never saw anything else. Not one human being.

It looked like we had this large island all to ourselves.

That was until we were woken by the sound of leaves and twigs breaking and some kind of mumbling.

I nudged John awake and had him listen as the noises became closer. Foolish me thought that maybe someone knew we were missing and was looking for us.

"We're over here!" I yelled. "Over here!" My voice sounded echo like and I was praying they found us.

Well, they found us all right. I'll tell you; it wasn't what we expected.

There were five of them. They looked like Indians. They were naked except for the covering over their crotch. Their faces were painted with white and red striped markings, and they were holding spears.

Well, it didn't take a rocket scientist to see this was not a good situation. They poked us in the chest with their spears as they spoke to us in a foreign language. A language John called mumble jumble or booga booga.

They were booga booga all right. We could tell by the tone in their voices they meant business. The others grabbed us by our arms and forced us to our feet. They looked at John's leg and saw he was hurt but they didn't seem to care. They made him walk on it anyway. All the while John crying and yelling from the pain.

They made us walk along a path that cut right through where we were sleeping for the last few days. Apparently, this looked like a path they walked regularly. It was dark and hard for us to see where we were going but they walked it as if they had special night vision.

I felt bad for John. He was crying in pain the whole time. Every once in a while one of the Indians smacked him in the head with their spear to shut him up. And he did for a while.

The Indians were taking us deeper and deeper into the woods that sounded more like a jungle. We could hear the night. Wolves, monkeys jumping from tree to tree making their chirping sounds.

My feet hurt and stung. I could tell they were getting all cut up they hurt so bad. I could the wet under my feet which caused me to slip on rocks and the branches sticking in my feet like splinter.

I tried to stop but the Indian kept hold of my shoulder keeping me up and made me keep going. I didn't have any idea where they were taking us but like I said, it didn't take a rocket scientist to know that they were up to no good.

Then I heard John crying so much he stopped. He couldn't go on anymore. Honestly, I was shocked that he made it this far. It's amazing how much the body can tolerate when under such stress.

The Indian mumbled something, which in his language was probably telling him to shut up and keep moving. He smacked John hard in the head with the spear that sounded like it broke his scull but it didn't. John was hard-headed. I know. Bad joke. When they saw John couldn't move any longer one of the other Indians picked him up and flung him over their shoulder and carried him the rest of the way.

All I could say was that the Indian carrying John had some amazing strength. He wasn't even big or muscular as one would expect but he carried him as he were nothing more than a sack of potatoes.

I never knew there were people out here like this. These Indians I mean. One would think where we are and the way the world has been that there would be no lands uninhabited. Let alone run into a bunch of Indians. I remember hearing stories about the amazon and the jungles of Panama but even that isn't what it used to be.

I could hear the sound of a water fall and soft drum beating as if in a ceremony. I knew we were getting closer to something not so good. I didn't have a good feeling about this. They were making this all too clear that they were up to no good.

I know this is bad but I remember at the time feeling really really mad at John for his decisions, for getting us in this mess in the first place. It wasn't like he wasn't worn. I know he's not the only blame. I blame myself. I have ever since this whole thing had ended just yesterday. I know my days are numbered. They did a number on us. They really did.

They pushed on the trail about another five hundred yards leading us into a camp.

There were hundreds of them!

About twenty of them were dancing around a large bon-fire, chanting in some language that sent shivers up my spine and a weird feeling around the back of my neck.

Something inside me told me to run. I pulled away but managed to only get about twenty feet until the Indian grabbed me. He grabbed my chin; his eyes were dark and bloodshot, and I felt like he were looking straight into me. He said something in a harsh voice which was probably something like, 'don't ever try that again,' Even though I couldn't understand him, I pretty much knew what he was saying.

Others came around as they saw us. They smiled from ear to ear. Weird though, the first thing I noticed was how their teeth were all black and rotten.

A little boy that looked to be around five grabbed a fistful of hair and yanked it. He yanked hard as if pulling on a rope. The way he giggled it was as if he were saying to the others, watch this.

A little girl was feeling my toes. Touching them one at a time as if she were playing this little piggy.

I yanked my foot away. She grabbed hold and pulled it back. She licked my toes and the bottom of my feet.

"Stop it! Stop it!"

She looked up at me and giggled. I felt like were their toys. At that moment I had no idea what they wanted with us. But when I realized what it was it made me scarier than anything ever had in this entire world. I mean, nobody can prepare you for something like this.

So awful.

There were large huts made of bamboo and grass all around us. It looked like that was what they lived in. Something like you would see on TV back in those jungle days or read about in National Geographic Magazine.

They threw us in a separate cage and tied it shut. John was in one and I in another. The bamboo bars were hard and did not move. They lashed them together very tight. It wasn't rope they tied them with it was some kind of silk like thread. Amazing how they built something so big and strong. To think we have to use engineers to build something like this.

Three children were having fun kicking a ball around. They played and laughed like any other kid would do. I couldn't keep from watching them. They weren't bothered by us being in here but only delighted in it. I felt like a caged dog.

John was lying on his back, gasping for breath and screaming in pain. His leg was bleeding bad.

The kids kicked their ball over toward me and it smacked into the cage I was in. That was when I saw it.

It wasn't a ball they were kicking around.

It was a scull. A human skull.

I screamed and jumped back. They thought it was funny and laughed and pointed as they said something to the others who also laughed.

I grabbed the bamboos rails and shook at them as hard as I could, screaming at them. Asking them what they wanted.

That only made them laugh more.

The little boy held the scull up and put it in my face and mumbled something as he moved it from side to side taunting me with it. All this taunting made the adults laugh more as if the kid were putting on a show.

Three of them pulled John out of the cage and lashed him to a table. John looked at me. I saw eyes filled with fear. Dread. They tied a rag over his mouth and just like that one of them sliced off his head.

John's body twitched and spasmed uncontrollably like a worm that had been chopped in two.

Blood gushed as they coated themselves with it as it collected in a small pit. Kids splashed around in it as we used to do when we played in a puddle. It was the most gruesome and disturbing thing I've ever seen.

I'll never forget that look in his eyes, staring at me even as his head was chopped off.

They then lifted him and placed him on a rack. I watched as they placed him on a grill and carried him over to the fire. By then John had stopped twitching. At least he didn't know what happened after.

I grabbed the scull the kids had been kicking around and pulled in from under the fence. In the back of the cage, I dug through the dirt like a dog. I could feel my fingernails tearing and my fingers hurt but I didn't care. I couldn't let them do this to me. At least the ground was muddy from all the rain we'd got earlier so I had that going for me. My plan was to get out of there before they came to me. I was going to be next on their menu.

I kept digging and digging making the most of the time I had while they were busy cooking John for a feast. Chances were they weren't going to try and do anything with me today. It was obvious they like their meat fresh.

I crawled under the hole I'd just dug when I heard one of them yell. I looked and saw him pointing at me as he warned the others.

I ran as fast as I could back toward that path which we came down. By this time, it was almost daylight so at least I was able to see a little bit of where I was going.

I'll tell you one thing for sure. They were some fast runners. One of them was upon me in no time. I turned and swung the scull and whacked him in the head. I knew I hurt him pretty good because he fell back and acted all dizzy like allowing me enough time to run.

I could hear them yelling behind me as they weaved between the trees like deer.

Another must've jumped from a tree because he seemed to have come from the sky. He got me to the ground, but I didn't give up there. I kept fighting.

I kicked and bit into his arm tearing off a large chunk. When he jumped back I whacked him in the face with the scull over and over until his face was all bloody.

I followed the trail over to the water thinking that if I could just get there I could hide. I thought that maybe that was my only chance.

I felt something sharp hit my back. I looked down and saw the point of the spear sticking out of my chest. It didn't hurt but it stung. Felt like a bad burn. Somehow, I'm not sure how I was able to do it, but I didn't let that stop me. I kept running and running.

With a bit of luck on my side I made it to the water and ran out as deep as I could go and started swimming away.

I saw them standing there on the island. Holding their spears as they watched me. Funny thing though. They didn't try to swim toward me like I thought they would. They just stood there staring.

I swam about another hundred yards then looked back at the island. That was when I saw it.

The strangest thing.

The island was fading away. Almost as if it were in a fog. Or a ghost. I didn't know what to think.

Then it was gone.

Gone as if it had never been there. Nothing but water.

I had no choice but to swim for it and I had no idea where I was going. The last thing I remembered I woke up here.

And I'm tired and I feel so weak. My heart is beating hard.

"JUST LIKE THAT SHE was gone?"

"Yep. The only one I ever talked to that survived the mystery island. As I've said before, a fisherman familiar with the area and the mystery island himself found her floating in the water. Sometimes he'll find something floating around out there and bring it back. We know where it came from. I tell people this story and they think I made it all up. Every year sailors and fishermen go missing and never heard from again. That is why, my friend. That woman managed to get off that island and I thank God that she did and shared this story because it confirmed what I was suspecting for a long time."

"That sure is quite a story."

"It is. Are you ready for that next drink?"

He chuckled. "After a story like that. I could use a couple more."

"HERE'S TO THE MYSTERY ISLAND."

240,000 MILES FROM NOWHERE

William held on for dear life as the ship pitched and rolled like a ship on the Atlantic Ocean.

Except they weren't on the Atlantic Ocean. They were in space.

On their large spaceship.

"What's all that beeping mean?" William asked. He was the CEO of a very large internet company called THE ZONE.

Red lights flashed all over the panel. This was followed by a series of ear-piercing and nerve-wracking alarms.

DONG DONG DONG DONG DONG

"What is that? "William asked, Bill Slater, who was helming the ship.

"I have no idea."

The ship shook and shuddered.

"I think something hit us. Charlie said. Charlie was the CEO of NIKRO, a popular pest country company.

"Not that I'm aware of," Slater said.

Slater, on the other hand was a famous actor William and Charlie hired who played a ship captain in a lot of Sci-Fi movies. He thought it was cool to pilot a real ship. As of now, he wasn't quite sure.

The three of them were on their way to the moon to check on some real estate in which to expand their businesses.

Slater saw something on the starboard side. It was large whatever it was. It wasn't an asteroid, and it wasn't another ship that was for sure.

The ship would've showed up on his radar. "That sure was weird. Never saw anything like that before."

"What was it?" Charlie asked.

"Not sure. It looked more like a shadow."

They were two days into the trip and according to plans they would be at the moon conducting business in the next twenty-four hours.

Unfortunately, things were not going as planned.

The fuel sensor light flashed.

Then the sensor that was supposed to tell the fuel sensor that something was wrong flashed.

Then the sensor that was supposed to tell all the other sensors that there was a problem in the sensor system didn't flash.

Instead, it showed in big red flashing letters MALFUNCTION.

"Well, that's just great," William said.

"We should pull into the space station and get this checked out," Charlie said. "No worries."

"Yes worries," Slater said. "This is the same exact problem they had with cars."

"What do you mean?" William said. He raised an eyebrow. He was a very optimistic person, probably too optimistic for his own good and wasn't known to accept defeat.

"I mean, according to the graph the space station is over three hundred thousand miles. We may not make it."

"Of course, we'll make it," Williams said slamming his fist on the table. "Don't say never. Never say never. I'm a pusher and a mover. We make things happen "

BONG BONG BONG BONG

Charlie cuffed his ears. "Somebody please shut off that alarm. I can't hear myself think."

"I'm doing the best I can," Slater said.

"Shouldn't you know these things?" William said. "We sent you to the best pilot schools in the nation."

Slater looked at William and raised a finger. "Let me remind you, sir, in case you forgot. You were the one that told the mechanic that we had a deadline and insisted that he repair it that same day. If I recall, he told you that there were still some more checks that needed to be conducted but you insisted, we leave on time. He recommended you give him two more days, but you threatened his job."

William's face turned red. "You have to put your foot up your employees' butts and get them moving if you want to get things done. You'll learn that one day when you get your own company."

"Maybe so but you don't treat your mechanic that way. Sal has been doing this for over twenty years. When your mechanic makes a recommendation, you'd be wise to follow his advice."

"You know, I can see a problem with you right now, Slater. You're going to let your employees walk all over you."

" Who's the three idiots on a spaceship that's malfunctioning?"

Charlie sat off to the side and remained silent with a look of doom on his face. "He's right, William. We should've listened to Big Sal."

"Sal was just trying to milk us for more time and money. All he had to do was replace a couple sensors and repair a few wires. How hard could that be?"

The ship shook and shuddered violently.

William held on to the rail. "Harder than we thought it would be, obviously."

More alarms went off. All red, yellow and blinking lights. The ship shook and shuddered as if it lost an engine or something.

They decided it would be best if they strapped themselves in and ride out the rest of the storm.

"This is so not good," Charlie said.

"Now, just calm your bones down. It's going to work out. This is the best ship money can buy."

"That's what they said about the Titanic," Charlie said.

"The Titanic was floating on water. We're in space."

"Which doesn't make it any safer," Charlie said.

"We're going be just fine."

The ship suddenly pitched to the port then quickly to starboard with such force that if they hadn't been strapped in, they would've been flung clear to the other side of the ship.

"What's going on, Slater? Talk to us," William said.

"Not good. Not looking good at all." His knuckles turning white as he held the helm. We are sooooooo screwed."

"I need you to be just a little bit more positive, Slater," William said.

Slater was doing his best to maneuver the ship but whatever was going on the ship was not cooperating and the ship went into a whirl spin, round and round they went. "You can think as positive as you want, Sir. But when you're screwed, you're screwed and it ain't making no difference."

The instrument panel went berserk with a bunch of BONG BONGS AND DING DINGS AND BUZZERS AND WHISTLES all coming together in a cacophony of sounds that told them this was some serious trouble.

There was a loud boom on the port side aft. The ship shook and shuddered. "I think that thing just hit us," Slater said.

"No worries," William said. " Nothing is going to damage this ship."

To make sure their ship was crash proof they made sure it was tested by the best of the best of rocket scientist.

The craft was at least two hundred feet long. Longer than the regular space shuttle. They wanted to make sure they had not only the best craft but the largest. Just like their nationwide corporate stores.

The craft had plenty of head room at seventy feet high with a wingspan of 90.06 feet and was well equipped with a fuel tank with the capacity to hold 600,000 gallons just in case they ran into some problems. They wanted to be sure they covered all angles.

Their plan was to get there and get themselves established. They'd spent the last fifteen years planning on where they were going to build and how they were going to do it. If they needed to get back to Earth, they would refuel at the International Space station.

Their stores would be able to provide services to anybody that moves to the moon and other near-by planets. Other travelers would be able to park their ships in one of their many hanger deck garages all equipped with the finest resting facilities and eateries. Of course, they had planned on supporting this program by charging a descent docking fee similar to crossing the bridges going into New York.

It was a no fail plan. They were excited about their future endeavors until....

"We're going to have to eject," Slater said.

"Eject? You mean like out there?" William asked.

"Afraid so."

The light to the starboard engine just malfunctioned. Then the port light for the port engine malfunctioned and again started beeping and buzzing.

"We've lost both engines?" Slater said.

Everything around them continued to spin at an uncontrollable rate at the speed of God knows what. The three of them felt nausea and dizzy and they could feel all the wine and lobster and steak dinner they had that afternoon rise from their stomachs.

Their heads throbbed and they were not doing well as they now list cabin pressure.

"Stand-by. We're ejecting," Slater tried to say but the speed of sound of which they were twirling around made it impossible to talk even with their helmets and suits on.

The canopy flew off at the push of the button. William and Charlie attached themselves with a long strap so they could stay together.

Charlie was the first to leave the ship and was nowhere to be found.

William and Charlie went up and up just as ship exploded into nothing but particles.

"That sure was a close one," William said.

"It was. Just in time I say."

The two of them were now floating around in space.

"Just when you think you've seen it all," William said. "I don't think we can get any further away than this. Slater, you there?"

"I'm here."

"Can you see us<" Charlie asked.

"No."

He had to be within at least five miles radius but out here that can seem like a very long way off.

"At least you can hear us," Charlie said.

"For now." He chuckled. It was one of those nervous chuckles that said that when you're screwed, you're screwed. "I don't think we're getting out of this one so easy this time."

William patted his pocket and felt the metal ring. "We have our GPS installed in our suits. It'll only be a matter of time before somebody finds us."

Charlie looked over at him. "Are you serious right now? Do you have any idea where we're at?"

"I know where we're at. I'm not an idiot. I'm telling you somebody will find us."

"This is outer space. The never-ending dark abyss. This isn't the Pacific Ocean. We're screwed, dude. Ain't nobody finding us."

"We're going to float around here till we die," Slater said.

"We're not going to die," William said. "I've paid good money for the best of the best GPS systems. Trust me."

Charlie chuckled. "Just like the ship?"

"Don't' be a wise guy."

"Ahhhh. I'm being serious right now. We're floating around out here in space cause our ship blew up. I haven't figured out yet if we're lucky or not."

"I say at this point we should've just stayed on the ship and blew up with it," Charlie said.

William and Charlie could hear him sniffle as if he were crying.

"I knew I shouldn't have listened to you," Charlie said. "Now you got us both killed."

"Not dead yet," Williams said.

"This is going to be a sad way to die," Charlie said. Floating around here till we starve to death or die of dehydration, whichever comes first."

"You have to think positive," William said. "You gotta be a pusher and a mover."

Charlie felt like reeling him in on the tandem line and punching him in the mouth. Right now, he wanted to get as far away from this idiot as possible. He thought no way was he going to stay attached to this guy until they die. "Please stop talking like that. Just stop."

"Talking like what?"

"All that positive thinking sales crap. Doesn't work."

"You too need to stop arguing," Slater said. "Just face the fact, we're screwed. Seriously screwed......... What is that?"

"Slater....." William said.

"Something is out here. Never saw anything like this......." Screams. "I knew I saw something out here."

"What is it?" Charlie's voice sounded shaky.

"It's big. Like some creature. Oh my God this is so awful." Screams...... "My leg. It just bit off my leg."

"Slater......" Williams said. "Hang in there. Slater! Slater!"

"My leg. Please make this thing stop. "It just ate off my other leg." More screams. Gurgles.

Silence.

"What do you think that was?" Williams asked.

"I have no idea. I know he said he saw something earlier after something banged into the ship."

"What else could be all the way out here in space."

"Scientist have been trying to explain that there may be other life forms out here."

"Sounded like it was some kind of monster," William said.

"Yeah. I know. Maybe we'll get lucky, and it won't find us."

"Ha. That's not likely. If it found him it's going to find us for sure."

"Maybe not."

Charlie pointed. "Look."

In the distance Charlie saw a large form. It was massive in size. It looked like a giant shark with big teeth, and it was coming right after them.

Don't miss out!

Visit the website below and you can sign up to receive emails whenever Christopher Ridge publishes a new book. There's no charge and no obligation.

https://books2read.com/r/B-A-RYTC-HZVGC

BOOKS2READ

Connecting independent readers to independent writers.

Also by Christopher Ridge

Hairy Scary Eight Legged Engineers
HOME INVASION
Bug Spray not Included
DateBite
Giant Steel Death Machines
The Ugly Truth About Shopping Carts
Dead End Job
Lobster Woman of Bubwater
Hatchet Hall
There's a Man on that Street
CUT'M UP TALES
Severance
The Fling
Macabrre Monthly
Strikeout
Splat
Slime
Because Google Said
Demented Tales
Captive
The Ghost Pirate
Clickety Clackers
Bumper to Bumper
The Hatch
Help Wanted

Creatures

Watch for more at creaturecritter.blogspot.com.

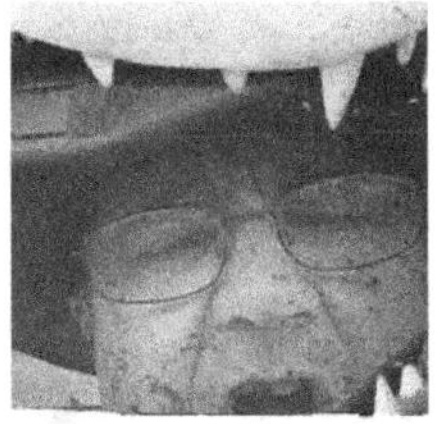

About the Author

Christopher Ridge is a creature feature horror and sci-fi writer. He enjoys B horror movies, aliens, monsters and mutant insects and such. To get an idea of what his stories and short novels are like think ATTACK OF THE KILLER TOMATOES, THEM, and IT CAME FROM OUTER SPACE. He lives in Indianapolis Indiana with his wife and two sons.

Read more at creaturecritter.blogspot.com.

www.ingramcontent.com/pod-product-compliance
Lightning Source LLC
Chambersburg PA
CBHW070823170726
48000CB00019B/2454